For Emilia
A. McA.

To my brother-in-law Jeremy Wernert
T. M.

This edition published by Parragon Books Ltd in 2014 and distributed by
Parragon Inc.
440 Park Avenue South, 13th Floor
New York, NY 10016
www.parragon.com

Text: © Angela McAllister 2007
Illustrations: © Tina Macnaughton 2007

ISBN 978-1-4723-8588-8

Printed in China

Little Doe

Angela McAllister

illustrated by Tina Macnaughton

Bath · New York · Cologne · Melbourne · Delhi
Hong Kong · Shenzhen · Singapore · Amsterdam

Little Doe was timid and shy.
She loved to nestle with her mother in their den at night,
but she was frightened of the big woods.

Every morning all the fawns
followed their mothers through the
woods to the meadows. Little Doe was afraid of
the rustling leaves and the creatures of the forest.

She was afraid to leap the ditch or cross the stream.
"Jump, Little Doe, jump!" the other fawns would cry.
But Little Doe would wait until they all moved on.
Then, slowly, she'd step across the stream alone.

When she reached the meadow Little Doe stayed
close to her mother and watched the others play.
If only she was brave enough to join in . . .

The other fawns loved to chase and hide but there
was one meadow where they would never stray . . .
It was the home of great **Giant Shadow Bird.**

No one had ever seen the Giant Shadow Bird.
They had only seen his **huge shadow**.
Sometimes he stretched out his long horns. Sometimes
he crouched small. All the fawns were afraid of him.
Little Doe wouldn't even dare peep through the trees.

Day by day the other fawns grew bold.
"Who will be the first to taste the grass
in the Giant Shadow Bird's meadow?" they said.
"I will," boasted one.
"Not before me," cried his brother.

Nobody asked shy Little Doe.

"I wish I was brave, Mama," Little Doe whispered that night.
"But you are," said her mother sleepily.
"Who me?"

"Yes." Her mother smiled.
"I know you are still frightened of the woods but you follow us every day,
even though you are afraid. And that is very brave indeed."
She licked Little Doe's ears.
"You can do whatever you want to do."

Little Doe lay awake watching the stars.
Could she really do whatever she wished?

Before dawn Little Doe crept silently out of the den and set off through the woods alone. Owls hooted. Night creatures scuttered through the leaves. The stream was icy cold.

Little Doe trembled.

She sniffed.

She listened.

But she went bravely on.

When she reached the meadow of the Giant Shadow Bird she
peered between the trees. The moon shone down but nothing
stirred. Little Doe took a step inside. She sniffed. She listened.

The meadow was empty.
"Oh," she sighed, "he's gone!"
Sleepy and disappointed, she lay
down alone and fell fast asleep.

Little Doe woke up feeling very hungry, and she began to eat.
The grass was so good she hardly noticed the sun rise. Suddenly
she heard frightened cries from the edge of the meadow.
Everyone had been searching for her.

"Little Doe! Watch out behind you!"

Little Doe turned...
A dark shape lay long in the grass, stretching out towards her.
"Run," the fawns cried. "Run, Little Doe, run!"

But Little Doe didn't run.
She saw what they couldn't see . . .

On the hill stood **a windmill,** stretching its **four arms** in the morning sun. With a creak the sails began to turn and below, its great shadow stirred too. The other fawns stepped nervously into the meadow. They laughed when they saw their mistake. "You are the bravest, Little Doe!" they agreed.

Little Doe's mother led them all into the sun.
"Run and play now," she said proudly.
And brave Little Doe sniffed the new morning,
smiled happily, and joined in the game.